caillou®

Just Like Daddy

Text: Christine L'Heureux • Illustrations: Claude Lapierre

chouette

Caillou is curious. He wants to know how
he was born. "Tell me," Caillou asks Daddy.
Daddy explains, "I was very much in love with
Mommy and we wanted to have a baby.
One day, you arrived!"

"Tell me more!" says Caillou. Daddy continues,
"When you were born, I was really happy.
Our eyes were the same color.
We were like two peas in a pod."
Caillou smiles.

"Then what?" asks Caillou. Daddy remembers. "You smelled so good. You loved it when I picked you up. You snuggled your little head into my shoulder." Caillou looks very pleased.

That evening, Caillou asks Daddy to show him the photo album. Daddy gets the album and shows him a picture. "Look, Caillou. That's you when you were a baby!" says Daddy. Caillou laughs. He looks so small!

Daddy shows him another picture.
"See, I was little too before
I became a daddy."
"You were a baby?" Caillou asks.
He is surprised. Daddy says proudly,
"When you grow up, you can be a
daddy too."

The next morning, Mommy asks Caillou to
wear his overalls. Caillou refuses.
He wants to wear a pair of pants and
his new belt. Mommy is puzzled.
"I want to dress like Daddy,"
Caillou explains.

Caillou is very proud to look like Daddy.
He goes all over the house carrying
a little suitcase full of toys.
Caillou is very busy, just like Daddy.

Today, Caillou is happy. Daddy gave him
a rake to help rake the leaves.
Caillou puts on a hat to protect himself
from the wind, just like Daddy.

Grandpa comes to help rake leaves.
"Grandpa, you're wearing a hat, too!"
says Caillou. Grandpa gives Caillou a kiss.
"That tickles!" laughs Caillou.

"You know, Caillou," explains Daddy,
"Grandpa is my daddy." Caillou is upset.
"No, he's my grandpa, mine!"
Grandpa smiles and says,
"Caillou, I'll always be your grandpa."

"You see, Caillou," adds Daddy,
"I'm your daddy, but I also have a daddy."
Caillou looks at him and says,
"When I grow up, I'm going to be
a daddy, too!"

We gratefully acknowledge the financial support of BPIDP, SODEC, and the Canada Council for the Arts for our publishing activities.

Text: Christine L'Heureux
Illustrations: Claude Lapierre

Canadian Cataloguing in Publication Data
L'Heureux, Christine, 1946-
Caillou, just like daddy
(North star)
Translation of: Caillou, comme papa.
For children aged 3 and up.

ISBN 2-89450-256-7

1. Childbirth - Juvenile literature. 2. Father and child - Juvenile literature.
I. Lapierre, Claude, 1942-   . II. Title. III. Series: North star (Montreal, Quebec).

RG525.5.L4513 2001   j612.6   C2001-940935-4

Printed in Canada
109876